£2

EGMONT
We bring stories to life

First published in Great Britain 2015 by Egmont UK Limited
The Yellow Building, 1 Nicholas Road, London W11 4AN

Written by Frank Tennyson
Edited by Emil Fortune
Designed by Richie Hull, Joe Bolder, Glen Downey
Illustrations by Robert Ball, Tsuneo Sanda and Ulises Farinas

© & ™ 2015 Lucasfilm Ltd.
ISBN 978 1 4052 7799 0
60311/5
Printed in Italy

To find more great *Star Wars* books, visit www.egmont.co.uk/starwars

Stay safe online. Any website addresses listed in this book are correct at the time of going to
print. However, Egmont is not responsible for content hosted by third parties. Please be aware
that online content can be subject to change and websites can contain content that is unsuitable
for children. We advise that all children are supervised when using the internet.

WELCOME
HUMANS

I am C-3PO, a protocol droid specialising in human-cyborg relations.

I am fluent in over six million forms of communication. Please allow me to translate for you! The information in this book was written in a wide variety of languages, from Galactic Basic to Huttese and Geonosian, but thanks to my advanced circuitry, it should now appear in your native tongue.

Inside you will find information on some of the galaxy's most famous planets, battles, heroes and villains, along with enough puzzles to baffle a military droid brain!

Now, if you won't be needing me, I'll shut down for a while...

THIS ANNUAL BELONGS TO:

NAME

- - - - - - - - - - - - - - - -

SPECIES

- - - - - - - - - - - - - - - -

HOME WORLD

- - - - - - - - - - - - - - - -

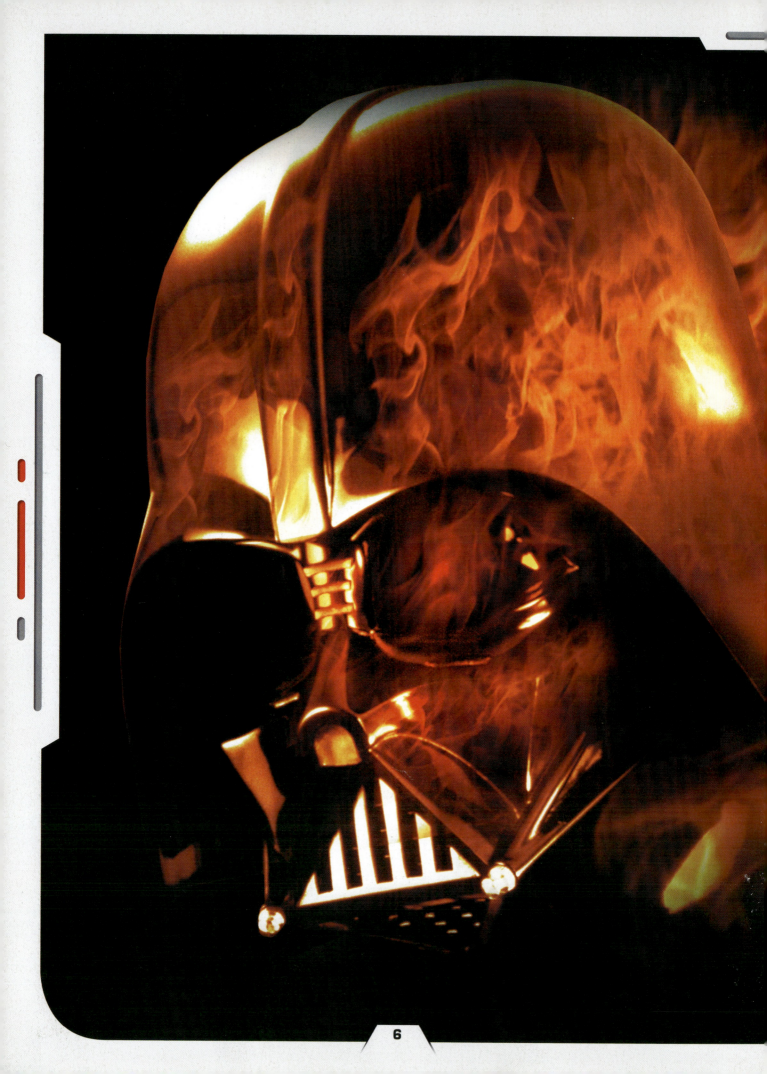

CONTENTS

JUMP TO LIGHTSPEED!

Han Solo's *Millennium Falcon* was one of the fastest ships in the Galaxy – despite its ramshackle looks.

NAVIGATE THE KESSEL RUN!

Han Solo once boasted that he completed the Kessel Run – a notorious and tricky smugglers' route – in less than 12 parsecs.

Can you complete the Run as fast as Han Solo and Chewbacca? Jump from point to point, adding the numbers on each path you travel down as you go. Cunning pilots can make it in 11 parsecs…

START

1   2

2   3   4   1

3   2   4   1   2   3

2   2   3   3   3   4

3   4   3   2

1   2

FINISH

GALACTIC
ATLAS

The *Star Wars* galaxy is an immense and varied place. Here are some of the most iconic planets and moons from the saga.

DAGOBAH

REGION OUTER RIM

TERRAIN SWAMP

This dark swamp-covered planet was teeming with life. Considered to be strong with the Force, Dagobah protected an exiled Yoda while discouraging unwanted visitors.

FAMOUS FOR:
On Dagobah, Master Yoda trained a young Luke Skywalker in the ways of the Force.

BEST QUOTE:
"Do. Or do not. There is no try" – Yoda tells Luke how to raise his X-wing from the swamp.

HOTH

REGION OUTER RIM

TERRAIN GLACIER FIELDS

This freezing ice planet was covered in thick snow and was home to wampas – fearsome, meat-eating predators. During the Galactic Rebellion, Hoth was the location of Echo Base, the Alliance's temporary HQ.

FAMOUS FOR:
An epic battle saw an Imperial assault take the base, though much of the rebel force escaped.

BEST QUOTE:
"There isn't enough life on this ice cube to fill a space cruiser" – Han Solo on Hoth's landscape.

TATOOINE

REGION OUTER RIM

TERRAIN DESERT

The desert home world of Anakin Skywalker and, later, his son Luke. Only parts of it could support life, and moisture farms were needed to extract water from the atmosphere. Luke was brought up by his aunt and uncle on such a farm.

FAMOUS FOR:
Slave boy Anakin was freed by Qui-Gon Jinn after winning a podrace on Tatooine. Many years later, Luke met Obi-Wan Kenobi and began his own journey towards becoming a Jedi.

BEST QUOTE:
"If there's a bright centre to the universe, you're on the planet that it's farthest from" – Luke tells the droids where they have landed.

CORUSCANT

REGION CORE WORLDS

TERRAIN CITY

This city-covered planet was the seat of government for the Old Republic. After Emperor Palpatine seized power, the Jedi Temple was converted into the Imperial Palace and Coruscant became the dark centre of the Empire.

FAMOUS FOR:
Anakin saving Palpatine from Windu's attack and completing his journey to the dark side of the Force.

BEST QUOTE:
"Execute Order 66" – On Coruscant, Palpatine issues the secret command for the Clone Army to exterminate all Jedi across the galaxy.

NABOO

REGION OUTER RIM BORDERS

TERRAIN SWAMPS, HILLS, PLAINS, CITIES

Inhabited by an amphibian race called Gungans and the peaceful Naboo, this planet was a stunning, lush and varied world – from the underwater cities to the majestic royal palaces.

FAMOUS FOR:
A three-way lightsaber fight between Darth Maul, Qui-Gon Jinn and Obi-Wan Kenobi.

BEST QUOTE:
"He is the Chosen One. He will bring balance. Train him" – Qui-Gon's dying speech to Obi-Wan

GEONOSIS

REGION OUTER RIM

TERRAIN DESERT

A desolate planet inhabited by insect-like creatures, Geonosis produced weapons and droids for the Separatists in the Clone Wars. It was also the scene of Jango Fett's death at the hands of Mace Windu.

FAMOUS FOR:

An astonishing duel between Count Dooku and his former master, Yoda.

BEST QUOTE:

"It is obvious that this contest cannot be decided by our knowledge of the Force, but by our skills with a lightsaber" – having defeated Anakin and Obi-Wan, Count Dooku prepares to duel Yoda.

MUSTAFAR

REGION OUTER RIM

TERRAIN VOLCANIC WASTELAND

A fiery planet with unstable volcanoes and lava rivers, Mustafar was an important mining facility. Later it would be host to a Separatist command centre.

FAMOUS FOR:

An incredible lightsaber duel between Obi-Wan and Anakin which took place throughout the facility and on the lava floods of Mustafar. Obi-Wan emerged victorious with Anakin suffering life-changing injuries.

BEST QUOTE:

"You were the chosen one! It was said that you would destroy the Sith, not join them. You were to bring balance to the Force, not leave it in darkness!" – Obi-Wan's lament after defeating Anakin.

YAVIN IV

REGION OUTER RIM

TERRAIN JUNGLE

The fourth moon of the planet Yavin was a lush, vibrant planet covered in jungle. It was here that the Rebel Alliance set up their first secret base, and plotted the destruction of the Imperial Death Star.

FAMOUS FOR:

Having identified a weak spot on the station, Rebel forces launched their attack from Yavin IV.

BEST QUOTE:

"You're all clear kid. Now let's blow this thing and go home" – Han clears the way for Luke's attack on the Death Star.

ALDERAAN

REGION CORE WORLDS

TERRAIN PLAINS, MOUNTAINS

Alderaan was a beautiful and peaceful planet which was one of the earliest supporters of the Rebel Alliance. Leia was the Princess of Alderaan and it was this which doomed the planet to destruction.

FAMOUS FOR:

Grand Moff Tarkin used the Death Star to destroy Alderaan, as a demonstration of the station's power and a warning to other planets sympathetic to the rebels.

BEST QUOTE:

"I felt a great disturbance in the Force, as if millions of voices suddenly cried out in terror and were suddenly silenced" – Obi Wan senses the obliteration of Alderaan.

FOREST MOON OF ENDOR

REGION OUTER RIM

TERRAIN FOREST

Home to the Ewoks, the low gravity on the forest moon of Endor meant that the trees grew to a vast size. The Galactic Empire established a shield generator to protect the unfinished second Death Star.

FAMOUS FOR:

The Battle of Endor where Ewoks and rebel soldiers combined to disable the shield generator. Alliance space forces then destroyed the Death Star II.

BEST QUOTE:

"Han will have that shield down. We've got to give him more time" – Lando Calrissian shows faith in his old buddy Solo.

KAMINO

REGION OUTER RIM

TERRAIN AQUATIC

Kamino was a secret world full of storms and tempestuous oceans. Cities on stilts housed a race of tall elegant beings called Kaminoans who were experts in cloning; it was on Kamino that the Republic's army of clone soldiers was produced.

FAMOUS FOR:

Bounty hunter Jango Fett and Obi-Wan going head to head on the landing platform.

BEST QUOTE:

"I'm just a simple man trying to make my way in the universe" – Jango underestimates his role in the *Star Wars* saga.

WHO ARE YOU?

Where would you fit in to the *Star Wars* universe? Take the quiz to find out!

1. The best ruler for the galaxy would be:

A. An elected Senate, in which everyone's point of view can be heard.

B. I don't mind, so long as they leave me alone.

C. A strong Emperor, who can provide peace and security through military might.

2. You receive a distress call from a broken-down freighter taking food supplies to a starving planet. Do you:

A. Help them repair their ship and escort them to the planet. That food is sorely needed.

B. Help them repair their ship – for a price. You need to eat, too.

C. Seize the cargo and sell it on the black market. Finders keepers.

3. The Trade Federation have blockaded your planet, and you can't leave in your starship. What do you do?

A. Negotiate with them. Perhaps you can convince them to let you leave.

B. Bribe an official to let you sneak through. There's always someone who'll take credits.

C. Their ships are no match for you. Just blast your way out.

4. While stranded on the planet Dathomir, you are confronted by a hungry rancor. What do you do?

A. Every living being is connected. Try and use the Force to calm the beast.

B. Have you seen the size of those things? Don't just stand there. Run!

C. You're hungry too, and a rancor could feed you for a week. Ignite your lightsaber.

14

5. You have discovered the location of a wanted criminal who is being hunted by the Hutts. What do you do?

A. Tell the authorities. The criminal will be brought to justice, not killed by gangsters.

B. See who will pay more – the criminal, to keep him safe, or the Hutts, as bounty.

C. Take the criminal's money for keeping him safe, then betray him to the Hutts and get paid twice.

6. You meet a group of Jawa scavengers who have droids to sell. You're interested in:

A. A protocol droid. Having a translator will be a big help with your diplomatic missions.

B. An astromech droid. You get in to plenty of scrapes, and your ship always needs repairs.

C. An assassin droid. They're illegal, but you have plenty of enemies to worry about.

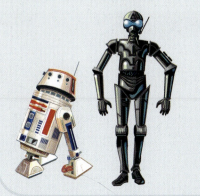

7. You are having a starship built to your specifications. What is your main requirement?

A. Maneuverability. You need a fast, agile ship that can out-fly attackers.

B. 'Special modifications'. Smuggling compartments, signal jammers, and hidden weaponry.

C. Massive firepower. Attack is the best form of defence, after all.

8. In a Mos Eisley back street, you are ambushed by thieves. How do you react?

A. Use the Force to persuade them to leave peacefully.

B. Hold them off with your trusty blaster pistol until you can escape.

C. Unleash Force Lightning on the pitiful fools.

MOSTLY A: The path of the Jedi is not an easy one, but you are making good progress. You are most like LUKE SKYWALKER

MOSTLY B: You try to do the right thing – as long as there's something in it for you. You are most like HAN SOLO

MOSTLY C: The dark side is strong in you. You are most like DARTH VADER

Swift, elegant and precise – a starfighter made for Jedi.

COCKPIT

Jedi starfighters had unusually large transparent cockpits, to maximise their awareness of the battle. Jedi pilots relied more on their Force-enhanced senses and agility than on electronic sensors and armour-plating.

R4 ASTROMECH

Every starfighter needs an astromech droid to make in-flight repairs and calculations. Obi-Wan Kenobi's faithful droid R4-P17 served with him in the Clone Wars, until she was lost in the Battle of Coruscant.

LONG-BARRELLED LASER CANNONS

The extreme length of these cannons gave them excellent range and accuracy, allowing the Jedi to pick off enemies with surgical precision. They could not be fired continuously, but with a Force-user in the pilot's seat one shot was usually enough.

ION CANNONS

Ion weaponry fired bursts of plasma which could disrupt a target's electrical systems. This was particularly useful against droid fighters, but having the ability to disable shields or engines meant that any ship could be captured or destroyed without the threat of retaliation.

KILL MARKINGS

Each of these markings represents one squadron of Separatist tri-fighters – deadly droid-controlled ships that could out-fly and out-shoot even the best living pilots. Taking them out was a priority for the Interceptors – and the source of a little competition between Jedi.

THE PATH OF A JEDI

How generations of children joined the mystical order of peacekeepers – from cradle to grave.

FIRST DISCOVERY

Microscopic life forms called midi-chlorians were the gauge of Jedi potential. They lived in living cells and communicated with the Force. A blood test – like the one Qui-Gon Jinn gave Anakin Skywalker – could reveal the level of midi-chlorians in a youngster's system. A high number suggested suitability for Jedi training.

EARLY STARTERS

The Council's reluctance to train Anakin Skywalker was due to the boy's future being "clouded" and Yoda sensing great fear in the boy. However, Anakin's age also counted against him: most recruits were infants. The Jedi Order kept careful records of Force-sensitive younglings, in a database called a holocron.

CENTRE OF LEARNING

Much of a youngling's training would take place in the Jedi Temple on the planet Coruscant. Here they would learn to wield lightsabers and immerse themselves in the Jedi Archive – a library containing the knowledge of every world and star system in the galaxy. Jedi had to learn wisdom as well as fighting skills.

TRAINING BEGINS

Young Jedi, or "younglings" began training using smaller lightsabers with safety blades. They would then progress to wearing vision-obscuring helmets which taught them to feel their surroundings and evade training remotes firing energy bolts.

MASTER AND APPRENTICE

When a student reached a certain standard of learning and understanding, he or she would be taken under the wing of a Jedi Master. There they would continue their development, going on missions and receiving on-job training.

USING THE FORCE

A key element of any Jedi's armoury was being able to manipulate objects using the Force. This helped them propel objects at opponents, knock them off their feet or block attacks. Jedi who were particularly strong in the Force could move objects as big as starfighters.

MIND TRICKS

Jedi could use the Force to convince weak-minded individuals they were telling the truth. Obi-Wan Kenobi used this trick on stormtroopers searching for the droids on Tatooine, while Luke gained access to Jabba's Palace by controlling the gangster's henchman Bib Fortuna.

BEYOND DEATH

Jedi maintained that death was not to be feared and was merely a part of the life cycle. Some Jedi could actually return as "Force spirits" after death. Qui-Gon Jinn was the first to learn the secret, and passed this knowledge on to Obi-Wan Kenobi, Yoda and Anakin Skywalker.

INSIDE A LIGHTSABER

A close-up look at the famous Jedi weapon

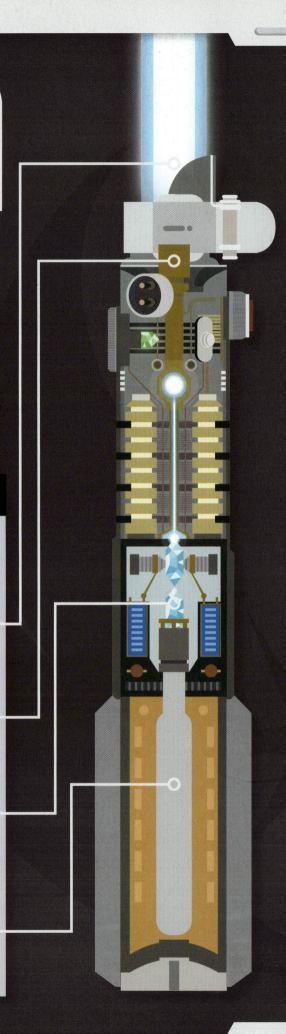

> "NOT AS CLUMSY OR RANDOM AS A BLASTER. AN ELEGANT WEAPON, FOR A MORE CIVILIZED AGE." – OBI-WAN KENOBI

LIGHTSABER USES

- Close combat and duelling
- Deflecting bolts from enemy weapons
- Cutting through blast doors

The blade of a lightsaber is a stream of super-heated plasma that loops back on itself.

The blade emitter – a lens mounted at the end of the hilt – converts the lightsaber's energy beam into a plasma blade.

A primary crystal and a focusing crystal concentrate energy into a powerful beam.

The special lightsaber battery can store huge amounts of energy and is virtually inexhaustible. Because the blade loops back into the hilt, it can be used to help recharge the energy cell.

DRAW GENERAL GRIEVOUS

This Jedi hunter loved lightsabers so much, he used four of them! Copy the fearsome cyborg in the space below.

WHERE'S THE WOOKIEE?

Chewbacca is being pursued by bounty hunters and has come to Mos Eisley spaceport. Can you find him in this busy crowd scene?

When you have found Chewbacca, see if you can spot Han Solo and Boba Fett!

See many more Wookiee hunts in the amazing new activity book *Where's the Wookiee?* – coming soon from Egmont!

RESCUE HAN!

Han Solo is encased in carbonite in Jabba the Hutt's fearsome palace. Which one of our heroes will reach him first? Follow the lines to find out.

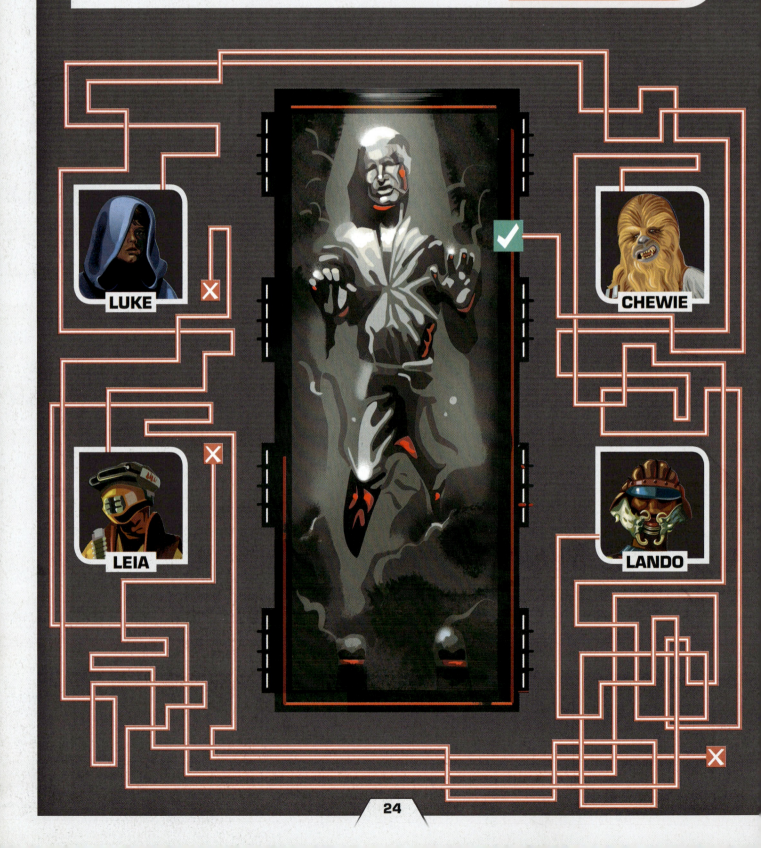

LUKE ✗

LEIA ✗

CHEWIE ✓

LANDO

24

DARK SIDE SUDOKU

Are you as fiendishly cunning as a Sith Lord? Try this dark side puzzle to test your wits …

Fill in the grid, making sure that there is only one of each character in each row, column, and 2x3 box. If you like, try drawing the missing characters in the blank squares.

	STORMTROOPER image, PALPATINE image	DRIOD	EMPRAR	GUARDIAN	Darth Vader image
DARTH VADER	Palpatine image	Guardian (red) image	GENAREL PALPETEME	Scout trooper image	Stormtrooper image
GENARAU PALPATO NE	DRIOD	Stormtrooper image	Darth Vader image	EMPRAR	GUARDIAN
GUARDIAN	Darth Vader image	Palpatine image	DRIOD	STORM TROOPER	Palpatine image
Palpatine image	STORM TROOPER	GENARA PALRITEI NE	Guardian (red) image	Darth Vader image	DRIOD
DRIOD	Guardian (red) image	Darth Vader image	STORM TROOPER	Palpatine image	EMPRAR

TOP FACTS
HAN SOLO

Everything you need to know about the super smuggler.

HAN SOLO WAS BORN ON CORELLIA

Corellia was a planet famed for its expert pilots and fast starships (like the *Millennium Falcon*). Bounty hunter Dengar also hailed from there.

HE WAS A NOTED SMUGGLER

On one run, Solo jettisoned his cargo in order to avoid arrest by the Imperial Navy. Because this was Jabba the Hutt's property, the crime lord placed a bounty on Han's head.

HE WAS "IN IT FOR THE MONEY"

Having helped Luke Skywalker to rescue Princess Leia from the Death Star, he took them to the Rebel Alliance. Han at first decided to not to join the planned attack on the space station, saying "What good's a reward if you ain't around to use it?"

"NEVER TELL ME THE ODDS." – HAN SOLO

HAN SAVED THE DAY

At the crucial moment in the Battle of Yavin, he had a change of heart and entered the fray. His intervention helped Luke destroy the Death Star and Han returned home a hero.

LUKE OWES HAN HIS LIFE

On the ice planet Hoth, Han braved vicious snowstorms to save an injured Luke from certain death. His decision to place Luke inside the carcass of his tauntaun was an ingenious, if smelly, masterstroke.

THE *MILLENNIUM FALCON* WAS WON IN A GAME OF CARDS

On Cloud City we learned that Han won the *Millennium Falcon* in a hand of Sabaac with fellow smuggler and gambler Lando Calrissian.

HE WAS BETRAYED BY HIS FRIEND LANDO

Fearful of the prospect of Imperial Forces taking over Cloud City, Lando did a deal with Darth Vader. He handed Han, Leia and Chewbacca over to the Empire. Han was then encased in carbonite to test the carbon-freezing process and given to Boba Fett to fulfil his bounty.

HAN WAS A HERO OF ENDOR

Han, Luke and Leia took a strike team to the forest moon of Endor. Their mission? To destroy the shields protecting the Death Star II. With a little help from the Ewoks they successfully defeated Imperial forces allowing Lando to obliterate the battlestation.

CHEWBACCA
AT A GLANCE

1 Chewbacca, or "Chewie" was a male Wookiee from the planet Kashyyyk

2 He was long considered a friend of the alliance and helped Yoda escape Palpatine's Jedi purge

3 Best friend to Han Solo, Chewbacca was an ace marksman and expert pilot

4 When Luke Skywalker met Chewbacca, the Wookiee was over 200 years old!

5 Chewbacca, like many Wookiees, was an excellent engineer, and helped keep the *Millennium Falcon* flying.

TOP 10
VILLAINS

From vicious gangsters to evil cyborgs, the *Star Wars* universe has more than its share of villains …

10 NUTE GUNRAY

Nute Gunray was Viceroy of the Trade Federation and part of a conspiracy with Sith Lord Darth Sidious, He led the invasion of Naboo and later planned the foiled assassination of Senator Amidala. Greedy and manipulative, the Neimoidian was killed by Sidious' new apprentice Darth Vader after he and the other Separatist leaders had outlived their usefulness.

9 STORMTROOPERS

Evil masterminds need enforcers, and the stormtrooper corps remain the most menacing and iconic foot soldiers ever. They were fanatically committed to the Emperor and his commanders. Their white battle armour still strikes fear into the hearts of their opponents, while specialist units including sandtroopers, snowtroopers and Imperial scout troopers wear their own distinctive garb.

8 GENERAL GRIEVOUS

This fearsome cyborg was trained in the art of lightsaber combat by Count Dooku. An accomplished Jedi hunter, he would use up to four sabers at once to overpower his victims. Grievous' formidable armour was not enough to save him from a spectacular end; Obi-Wan Kenobi tore open his chest plate and fired a blaster into the villain's heart.

7 JANGO FETT

Jango Fett was the genetic template of the Clone Army which destroyed the Jedi Order. However, his effect on the galaxy extends way beyond that. Jango was a bounty hunter of huge reputation, using an arsenal of weapons and intimidating armour to capture fugitives in exchange for cold, hard cash. His death at the hands of Mace Windu had grave consequences for his cloned 'son', Boba Fett.

6 JABBA THE HUTT

Jabba was a gangster renowned for running criminal activities throughout the entire galaxy. Most famously, he placed a price on Han Solo's head after the smuggler jettisoned one of Jabba's illegal shipments when threatened by an Imperial Cruiser. Bounty hunter Boba Fett eventually captured Solo and delivered him to the slug-like alien. However, this would prove a fateful move as Luke Skywalker, Princess Leia and Lando Calrissian rescued Han and Jabba met a gruesome end.

5 COUNT DOOKU

Trained by Yoda, Count Dooku left the Jedi order to become Darth Sidious' second disciple. His plan was to build a Sith army with Anakin Skywalker as their commander. In their first battle, Dooku sliced off Anakin's arm, such was his superior experience and duelling skill. In their second encounter, the story was very different. A much more powerful Anakin tapped into his dark side and killed Dooku – one Sith Lord to be replaced with another.

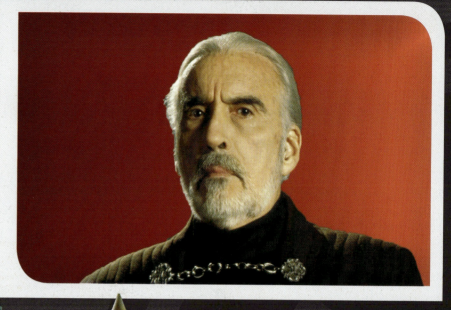

4 BOBA FETT

Boba was a clone of Jango Fett, raised as his son and taught all the skills of his "father". Learning hand-to-hand combat, using the deadly weaponry at his disposal and later witnessing the demise of Jango at the hands of Mace Windu, transformed a boy into a lethal fighting machine. The legendary bounty hunter was one of the villains who imprisoned Han Solo in carbonite.

3 DARTH MAUL

Darth Maul was Darth Sidious' first apprentice. A formidable warrior, the Zabrak from Dathomir brought down Jedi Master Qui-Gon Jinn using his trademark double-bladed lightsaber. Obi-Wan Kenobi avenged Qui-Gon by cutting the Sith Lord in two at the culmination of an epic battle. However, Maul would prove a difficult opponent to destroy …

2 EMPEROR PALPATINE/ DARTH SIDIOUS

Despite his image as a noble and compassionate political leader, Chancellor Sheev Palpatine was in fact Darth Sidious, Dark Lord of the Sith, intent on ending the Jedi Order and declaring himself ruler of the galaxy. The recruitment of Anakin Skywalker as a Sith was his greatest achievement but also his downfall. The Emperor used Vader to quell a rebellion – but it was an uprising of a different sort that brought him to his doom.

1 DARTH VADER

Once a famous Jedi Master, Anakin Skywalker fell under the thrall of the dark side to become an all-powerful Sith Lord. He almost destroyed the Rebel Alliance but the sight of his son suffering at the hands of the Emperor saw the remaining good in him rise to the surface. Vader threw his former master down the Death Star's reactor shaft and, although, he received mortal wounds, his redemption meant one of the most feared men in the galaxy ultimately died a hero.

DARTH VADER

Getting under the armour of the Dark Lord

FIRST ENCOUNTER

Discovered by Jedi Master Qui-Gon Jinn and his Padawan Obi-Wan Kenobi on Tatooine, a ten year-old Anakin Skywalker showed rare courage by taking part in the Boonta Eve Classic podracing event. His victory secured the parts the Jedi needed for their starship.

THE CHOSEN ONE

Anakin's blood was found to be rich in midi-chlorians, a microscopic life form that allowed beings to use the Force. Qui-Gon's calculations led him to believe that Anakin was the "Chosen One", an individual who would bring balance to the Force.

JEDI IN TRAINING

A talented but brash apprentice, Anakin was trained in the way of the Force by Obi-Wan but was soon influenced by Chancellor Palpatine to become suspicious of the Jedi Order.

> "YOU DON'T KNOW THE POWER OF THE DARK SIDE." – DARTH VADER

A DARK PATH

Anakin's mother died after being kidnapped by Tusken Raiders. Overcome with rage, he took a brutal revenge on the Sand People.

FEAR TURNS TO HATE

Anakin foresaw the death of his beloved Padme in his dreams. Palpatine – Darth Sidious in disguise – used this fear to turn him to the dark side of the Force.

FIRST MISSION

Sidious dubbed Anakin Darth Vader and gave him his first task – to go the Jedi Temple with a squad of clone troopers and slay all the Jedi.

ULTIMATE DUEL

Anakin's first battle with Obi-Wan on Mustafar ended in a dramatic defeat. Both legs and an arm were severed and he suffered horrific burns. Treated at a Surgical Reconstruction Centre on Coruscant, he awoke to find himself with artificial limbs and encased in an armoured life-support suit.

I AM YOUR FATHER

The most feared figure in the universe, Vader revealed himself as Luke Skywalker's father. Ultimately this bond would see him destroy the Emperor and bring balance to the Force.

A JEDI'S END

Killed during his assault on the Emperor, Anakin was cremated in the manner of a Jedi, and appeared to his son in spirit form alongside Obi-Wan and Yoda.

DEATH STAR
CROSSWORD

Test your knowledge with this fiendish trivia puzzle - all the answers are in this book

ACROSS

3 Former owner of the *Millennium Falcon*, _____ Calrissian (5)

5 Trade Federation Viceroy _____ Gunray (4)

7 Imperial soldiers (13)

9 Trade organisation which invaded Naboo. (10)

11 Order who used the dark side of the Force. (4)

14 The colour of Darth Vader's blade (3)

16 *The _____ Menace.* (7)

17 R2-D2 is a _____. (5)

18 Trooper made from the DNA of Jango Fett. (5)

19 The city where Luke Skywalker learned Darth Vader was his father. (5)

DOWN

1 The highest rank obtainable by a member of the Jedi Order. (6)

2 Qui-___-Jinn, who was mentor to Obi-Wan Kenobi (3)

4 Abbreviation for All-Terrain Armoured Transport (2-2)

6 Padme, the Queen of Naboo. (7)

7 The (illegal) profession of Han Solo. (8)

8 The small furry creatures who helped the rebels in *Return of the Jedi*. (5)

10 Once home to Princess Leia, the planet destroyed by the Death Star. (8)

12 "Fear leads to anger, anger leads to ____." (4)

13 A power that "surrounds us and penetrates us. It binds the galaxy together". (5)

15 The planet whose forest moon is inhabited by 8 down. (5)

16 A young Anakin Skywalker beat Sebulba in this sport to earn his freedom. (9)

1
2 GO
3 LANDO
4
5 NUTE
6
7 STORMTROOPERS
7 SMUGGLER
8 EWOK
9
10
11 S
12 HATE
13
14 RED
15 ENDOR
16 PODRACING
17 DROID
18
19 CLOUD

HUTT FLATS

START HERE!

MOS ESPA

Engine blows up! Miss a turn fixing it

Swerve to avoid a rocky pillar! Go back one space

MUSHROOM MESA

Full speed! Go forward two spaces

THE BOONTA EVE CLASSIC

Get ready for the most thrilling event of the Tatooine podrace season!

RULES

- You will need one counter for each player, and one die.
- Each player rolls a die to see who goes first.
- The highest roll wins. If it is a tie, roll again.
- The player on the first player's left goes next, and so on.
- Each turn, roll the die and move that number of spaces. Follow any instructions in the square you land on.
- If you land on another player's square, both of you must roll a die. The lowest scoring player misses a turn.
- The first player to complete three laps of the circuit wins. You must pass Mos Espa to complete a lap.

Shot at by Sand People snipers – miss a turn

Boost out of the canyon – roll again

Hit the sides! Go back one space

THE CORKSCREW

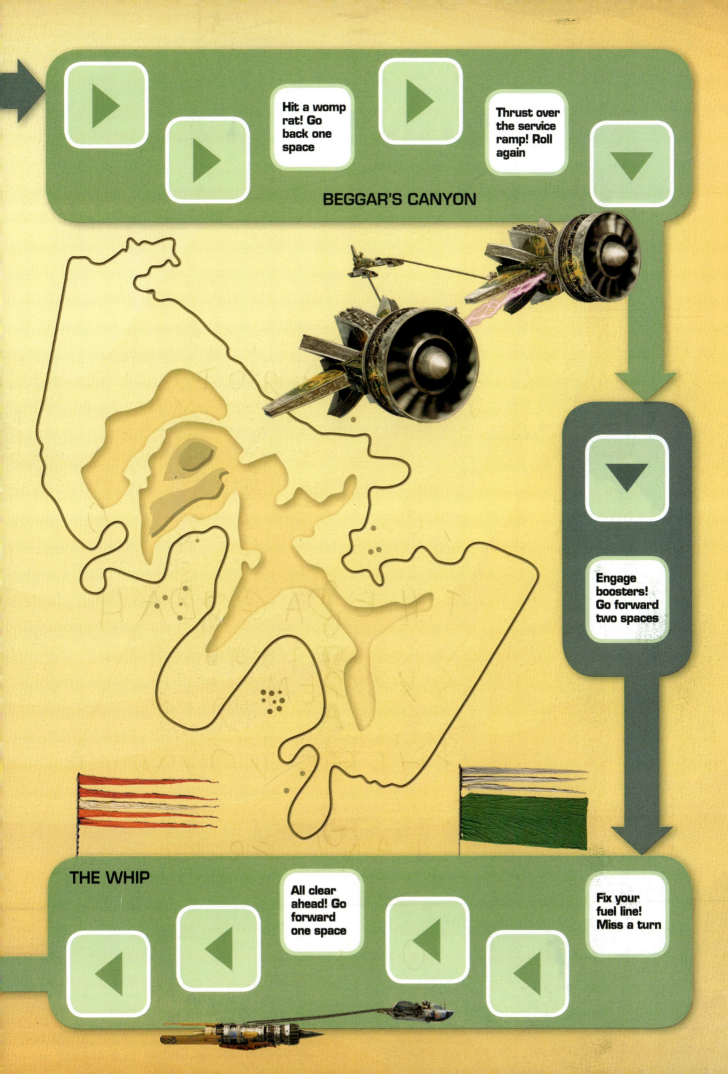

Hit a womp rat! Go back one space

Thrust over the service ramp! Roll again

BEGGAR'S CANYON

Engage boosters! Go forward two spaces

THE WHIP

All clear ahead! Go forward one space

Fix your fuel line! Miss a turn

OBI-WAN'S MESSAGE

The spirit of Obi-Wan Kenobi has a message for Luke. Can you decode it using the key below?

A	B	C	D	E	F	G	H	I	J	K	L	M

N	O	P	Q	R	S	T	U	V	W	X	Y	Z

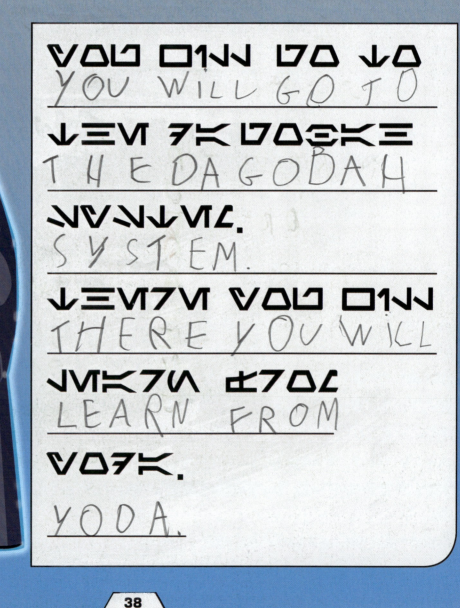

YOU WILL GO TO

THE DAGOBAH

SYSTEM.

THERE YOU WILL

LEARN FROM

YODA.

MAZE MASTER

Following Obi-Wan's orders, Luke arrives at a mysterious planet. Help him find a way through the maze to where a Jedi Master awaits him.

START

YODA!

YODA

LEGENDARY STATUS

Small in size but a giant among Jedi, Yoda was wise, powerful in the Force and a skilled lightsaber combatant. He trained Jedi for over 800 years.

FIGHTING STYLE

Yoda was a master of the Ataru lightsaber form which involves Force-assisted acrobatics, such as somersaults and leaping strikes.

FEEL THE FORCE

Yoda could move large objects at will, once lifting Luke Skywalker's X-wing out of a swamp and even causing enemy ships to collide during the Battle of Coruscant.

A SENSE OF FOREBODING

Yoda was reluctant to allow a young Anakin to be trained as a Jedi Knight because he sensed great fear in the boy, saying: "Fear is the path to the dark side. Fear leads to anger. Anger leads to hate. Hate leads to suffering."

MASTER TEACHER

The evil Count Dooku was once Yoda's Padawan and Obi-Wan Kenobi also learned from the great Jedi as a youngling.

AN OLD FRIEND RETURNS

Yoda heard the voice of Qui-Gon Jinn from beyond the grave and the fallen Jedi led him on a journey of discovery. It was through this revelation that Yoda unlocked the secret of Force immortality.

INTO EXILE

After an epic fight with Darth Sidious, Yoda chose to go into exile on the swamp planet Dagobah. It was here, many years later, that he trained Luke Skywalker to become a Jedi.

END OF THE JOURNEY

Yoda's last words were "Luke. There is another Skywalker," referring to Princess Leia.

SLAVE I

Boba Fett's deadly spaceship is full of surprises.

ROTATING COCKPIT

Slave I flies in an upright position, but lands on its 'back'. The cockpit rotates to keep the pilot the right way up at all times.

REPULSORLIFT WINGS

Slave I is an unusual craft which requires a lot of skill to fly effectively. The ship's swivelling wings help stabilise it in flight and during takeoff and landing, and must be carefully controlled.

HIDDEN ION CANNON

Boba Fett continued to modify *Slave I* after inheriting it from his clone 'father', Jango, adding all kinds of secret and often illegal systems. The concealed ion cannon could be used to disable unsuspecting ships; a powerful tractor beam could then reel his prey in. Other hidden tricks included torpedo launchers and cloaking systems.

ACCESS RAMP

Access to the inside of the craft is via a retractable ramp. Weapons in the tail section can provide covering fire if *Slave I* lands in a combat situation.

TWIN BLASTER CANNONS

The only visible weapons are these twin short-range blasters – which still pack quite a punch.

OBI-WAN KENOBI

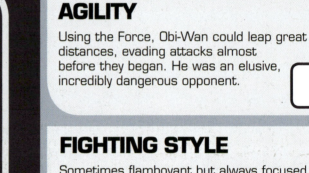

AGILITY

Using the Force, Obi-Wan could leap great distances, evading attacks almost before they began. He was an elusive, incredibly dangerous opponent.

FIGHTING STYLE

Sometimes flamboyant but always focused and cunning, he was a master of working out his adversaries' weaknesses and taking maximum advantage of them.

INTELLIGENCE

Obi-Wan was a wise and accomplished strategist and spy. However, his friendship with Anakin Skywalker blinded him to a growing menace from within the Jedi Order.

WEAPONS

The lightsaber was the weapon of choice for all Jedi, and Obi-Wan used his as an extension of mind and body. Add this to his manipulation of the Force, and he represented a formidable foe.

VEHICLE

Obi-Wan was a skilled pilot, but despite taking the helm of the likes of a *Radiant VII*, a Jedi Interceptor and even a bongo sub, he was not associated with any specific vehicle.

"THERE ARE ALTERNATIVES TO FIGHTING." – OBI-WAN KENOBI

TOTAL SCORE

BOBA FETT

Who would win in a showdown between these *Star Wars* legends? Give them each scores ...

AGILITY

As a clone of the bounty hunter Jango Fett, Boba was literally born for combat. He was heavily armoured but, thanks to his jet pack, moved with deceptive speed.

FIGHTING STYLE

Direct, uncomplicated and merciless, Boba used superior firepower to overwhelm his opponents. Expert in hand-to-hand combat and able to take to the air, he was the complete fighting machine.

INTELLIGENCE

Boba tracked down prey all over the galaxy, using deductive skills and reasoning. Anyone who could work with, and for, Darth Vader but still survive, was a very shrewd operator indeed.

WEAPONS

A one-man arsenal, Boba had a variety of weapons at his disposal including a flamethrower, a sonic beam, boot spikes and his iconic EE-3 blaster rifle.

VEHICLE

The deadly *Slave I* was passed on to Boba from his 'father' Jango. He fitted it with more cannons and torpedoes – but arguably its biggest weapon was the fear associated with its infamous owner.

"HE'S NO GOOD TO ME DEAD." – BOBA FETT

45

PUZZLE PROTOCOL

Can you solve these fiendish droid logic puzzles?

Try the easy ones, then move up to Level 2!

- There must be an equal number of R2-D2s and C-3POs in each row and column
- There can never be more than two R2-D2s or C-3POs next to each other

LEVEL 1

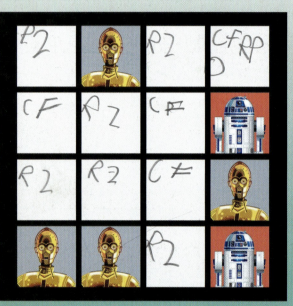

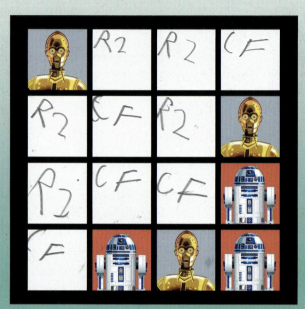

LEVEL 2

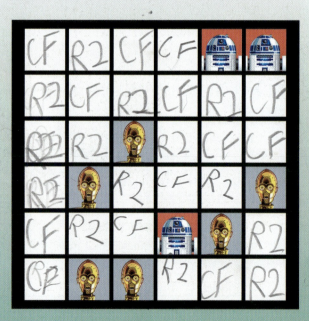

DROID WORD SEARCH

Star Wars is full of all kinds of droids. Search for the droid-related words in the grid – they can run up, down, backwards or diagonally.

C	C	I	R	C	U	I	T	Q	Y	H	N	H
N	X	A	S	S	A	S	S	I	N	B	A	V
E	M	Y	E	L	M	N	C	Z	A	S	J	A
L	W	S	B	Z	A	H	R	T	S	P	C	S
O	E	Z	O	I	O	C	T	D	O	I	T	T
C	F	D	R	P	O	L	I	B	H	D	H	R
O	G	V	P	C	E	D	G	D	F	E	R	O
T	O	E	U	R	Y	Z	N	G	E	R	E	M
O	R	T	G	L	O	A	J	A	O	M	E	E
R	B	Q	R	J	T	G	Y	R	M	O	P	C
P	J	U	Y	A	S	U	R	K	I	M	I	H
H	L	Z	Z	E	L	J	R	A	H	W	O	I
J	X	G	R	Z	C	Q	G	E	M	M	S	C

FIND THESE DROIDS

ARTOO
ASSASSIN
ASTROMECH
BATTLE

BUZZ
CHOPPER
CIRCUIT
COMMANDO

MEDICAL
PROBE
PROGRAM
PROTOCOL

SPIDER
THREEPIO
VULTURE

IMPERIAL CODE

Garindan is an Imperial spy on Tatooine – and he has some important coded news for his masters.

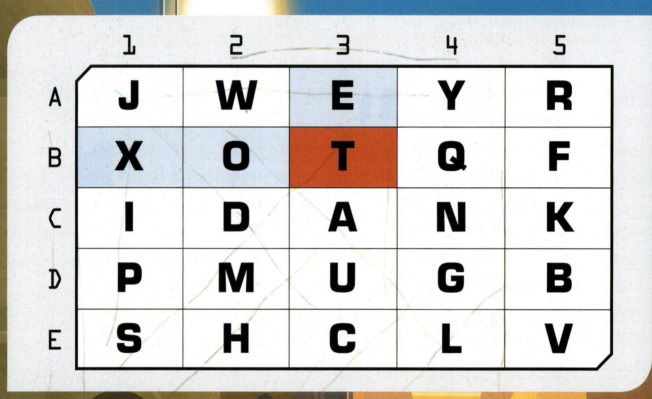

	1	2	3	4	5
A	J	W	E	Y	R
B	X	O	T	Q	F
C	I	D	A	N	K
D	P	M	U	G	B
E	S	H	C	L	V

Decode the message by finding the letter in the grid for each pair of coordinates. For example, 'B3' refers to the letter 'T', as above.

B3-E2-A3   A5-A3-D5-A3-E4-E1

_____

C3-A5-A3   C3-B3   B3-E2-A3

_____

C2-B2-E3-C5-C1-C4-D4   D5-C3-A4

_____

SCUM AND VILLAINY

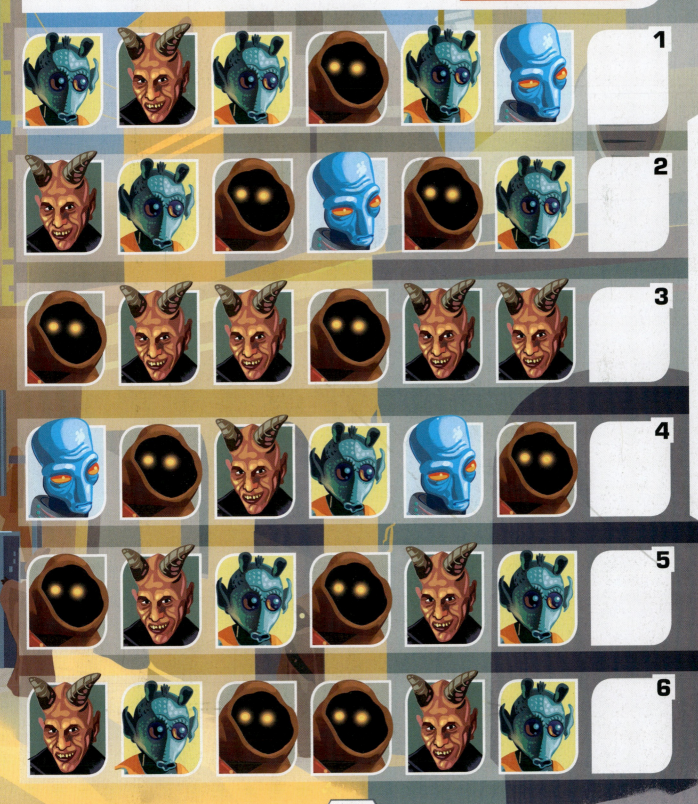

49

X-WING

> The iconic starfighter helped win many battles for the Rebel Alliance

COCKPIT

Equipped with a state-of-the-art targeting computer – though some pilots, like Luke Skywalker, preferred to use the Force.

ION ENGINES

Four ion engines which could be independently controlled made the X-wing hugely agile in a dogfight.

R2 ASTROMECH

Luke Skywalker's trusty companion R2-D2 flew many combat missions with him.

S-FOILS

In combat, the X-wing's S-foils would be opened out into attack position. This gave the cannons a wider firing range.

LASER CANNONS

Four laser cannons designed to give maximum range and firepower. The X-wing could destroy many enemy starfighters before they could get close enough to shoot back.

TOP VEHICLES
TIE INTERCEPTOR

COCKPIT

TIE fighter pilots must wear spacesuits – the TIE series sacrifices life support in favour of firepower.

LIGHTWEIGHT DESIGN

TIE fighters do not carry shields, armour or a hyperdrive – a single shot can destroy them, and they are designed to operate from a command ship or space station. What they lack in defences, they make up for in speed and weaponry.

CUTAWAY WING DESIGN

Sections cut out of the solar panels on each side of the cockpit allow the pilot a wider field of view, and makes the entire craft lighter and more agile.

EXTRA LASER CANNON MOUNTS

Two more cannons could be mounted beneath the cockpit – where the cannons are positioned on a TIE fighter – giving a total of six guns. This made the interceptor the most heavily-armed fighter in the Imperial Fleet.

WINGTIP BLASTER CANNONS

The TIE interceptor features four blaster cannons mounted on the wings, giving it a huge advantage over earlier models.

TOP FACTS
DARTH MAUL

Everything you need to know about the scary Sith Lord.

DARTH MAUL WAS BORN ON THE PLANET DATHOMIR

The infant Dathomirian was destined to become a slave to the Nightsisters, a magical branch of the dark side, but his mother elected to give him to Darth Sidious.

SIDIOUS' FIRST APPRENTICE

The Sith 'Rule of Two' states there are only ever two Sith Lords at a time – a master and an apprentice, who is encouraged to surpass and destroy their master.

MAUL BROUGHT A MYTH TO LIFE

Before the events of *The Phantom Menace*, few thought that the Sith still existed. However, when he revealed himself as part of the plot to bring down the Republic, the legend became frighteningly real.

A LIGHTSABER WITH A DIFFERENCE

Jedi and Sith would create their personalised lightsabers to match their abilities and personalities. Darth Maul's invention was a double-bladed weapon which could act as both a sword and staff.

HE LOVED DESTROYING JEDI

When two Jedi – Obi-Wan Kenobi and Qui-Gon Jinn – rescued Queen Amidala of Naboo, Maul relished the challenge to intercept. Killing Jedi was his life's mission.

Get colouring and bring Darth Maul to life

AN EPIC BATTLE ENSUED

After an initial skirmish, Maul met his prey on Naboo with dramatic consequences. The Sith's incredible agility and skills were a match for the two Jedi and he struck Qui-Gon down.

OBI WAN'S VENGEANCE

Seemingly defeated by Maul and hanging on to the edge of a reactor shaft, Obi-Wan used the force to summon Qui-Gon's lightsaber. Leaping into the air he cut Maul in half who fell to his "doom".

BACK FROM THE DEAD

Maul returned during the Clone Wars having survived his bisection. Now a cyborg with first a spider-like lower-half and then later more humanoid robotic legs, he teamed up with his brother Savage Opress.

THE RULE OF TWO

Having tried and failed to destroy Obi-Wan, Maul and Savage had a colossal battle against his one-time master. Darth Sidious killed Savage and told Maul he had been replaced by another apprentice – but left the Zabrak villain alive.

TOP 10
DUELS

Some of the most significant moments in the history of the Galaxy were small but epic duels ...

10 OBI-WAN KENOBI VS JANGO FETT

ATTACK OF THE CLONES

On the secret world of Kamino, Obi-Wan discovered an army of clones created from legendary bounty hunter Jango Fett. Cue a battle featuring Jango's blaster, torpedoes and jet pack versus Obi-Wan's lightsaber and Force abilities. Ultimately Jango escaped but not before a homing device was placed on his ship, the *Slave I*.

9 YODA VS COUNT DOOKU

ATTACK OF THE CLONES

A shuffling, aged Yoda transformed into an athletic fighting machine in this encounter. First using the Force to repel Dooku's attack of flying debris and lightning bolts, the 900 year-old fought his former Padawan to a standstill with his lightsaber. It was only when Dooku distracted Yoda by almost crushing Anakin and Obi-Wan that the Count was able to flee.

8 OBI-WAN KENOBI VS GENERAL GRIEVOUS

REVENGE OF THE SITH

What to do when faced with a foe armed with four lightsabers? Its easy if you are a Jedi with Obi-Wan's advanced training and skills. First you sever two of the laser-sword-wielding robotic hands, then engage in a jaw-dropping chase and take on your opponent in hand-to-hand combat. Even when you are seemingly overpowered, you find a way to rip open their chest plate and fire a blaster into a cyborg heart. Simple.

7 MACE WINDU VS SENATOR PALPATINE

REVENGE OF THE SITH

Aware of his treachery, Windu and fellow Jedi Masters Kit Fisto, Agen Kolar and Saesee Tiin arrived to arrest Palpatine. After Windu's companions were killed, Windu seemingly won an exhausting duel. When Windu was about to put the Sith master to the sword, Anakin intervened, cutting off the Jedi's hand and allowing Palpatine to send Windu falling to his death.

6 OBI-WAN KENOBI AND QUI-GON JINN VS DARTH MAUL

THE PHANTOM MENACE

This duel between Obi-Wan, Qui-Gon and Darth Maul had everything – fantastic sword play, amazing acrobatics, use of the Force and of course the Sith Lord's unique double-bladed lightsaber. After Qui-Gon was killed by Maul, Obi-Wan launched a furious attack, only to face defeat himself by falling into a melting pit. Using all his training, Obi-Wan leapt from the pit, summoned his Master's lightsaber and cut Maul in two.

5 OBI-WAN KENOBI VS DARTH VADER

A NEW HOPE

Obi-Wan had shut down the Death Star's tractor beam when he came face to face with former pupil Darth Vader. An iconic lightsaber battle ensued. "If you strike me down I will become more powerful than you can possibly imagine", said the Jedi; Obi-Wan allowed Vader to destroy him but his body mysteriously vanished; his spirit survived through the power of the Force.

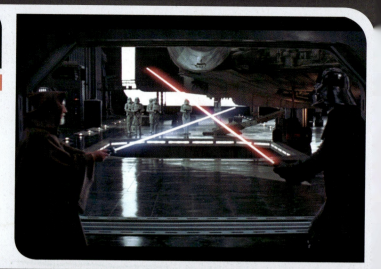

4 LUKE SKYWALKER VS DARTH VADER

RETURN OF THE JEDI

The second Death Star was the location of yet another stunning lightsaber duel – this time between father and son. Enraged by Vader's threat to turn his sister Leia to the dark side, Luke unleashed a vicious assault, severing the Sith's hand but refusing to take Vader's life. Furious, the Emperor unleashed Force lightning upon Luke. Seeing his son in mortal danger, Vader turned away from the dark side and killed his former master, throwing him down a reactor shaft.

3 YODA VS DARTH SIDIOUS

REVENGE OF THE SITH

The showdown between Sidious and Yoda did not disappoint. The battle commenced with both being thrown across the room by their opponent's Force powers. Then an intense lightsaber duel progressed into the Senate Chamber, where Sidious hurled Senate pods towards Yoda. Another confrontation of Force powers saw the combatants blasted apart from one another. With no clear winner, Yoda exiled himself to Dagobah and Sidious went to Mustafar to rescue the injured Anakin.

2 OBI-WAN KENOBI VS ANAKIN SKYWALKER

REVENGE OF THE SITH

Channelling the rage that had consumed him, Anakin wore down his opponent in a battle that progressed through a mining plant and on to the lava fields of the fiery planet Mustafar. When seemingly fated to die at the hands of his former friend, Obi-Wan leapt off the floating platform to the safety of a sand bank. Anakin ignored his plea not to try and assault the higher ground and paid the price, losing his left arm, both legs and suffering terrible burns.

1 LUKE SKYWALKER VS DARTH VADER

THE EMPIRE STRIKES BACK

"I am your father". When Darth Vader uttered that immortal line, it was not just Luke Skywalker who was rocked to his core – everyone captivated by the *Star Wars* story experienced that same moment of shock. Before the revelation, we were witness to a fierce fight between a Sith Lord and apprentice Jedi on Cloud City. It was clear from early on that Vader was the superior warrior and he used advanced swordsmanship and Force abilities to overcome his inexperienced but talented foe. The climax to their battle saw Vader sever Luke's hand and reveal their true relationship. Never before or since have four words transcended popular culture and sent generations of movie fans into delirium.

SAY WHAT?

Match the famous *Star Wars* quotes to their characters.

1 "This is our most desperate hour. Help me, Obi-Wan Kenobi. You're my only hope."
ANSWER

2 "Hokey religions and ancient weapons are no match for a good blaster at your side."
ANSWER

3 "Now, witness the firepower of this fully armed and operational battle station!"
ANSWER

4 "Help! I think I'm melting! This is all your fault!"
ANSWER

5 "Fear leads to anger. Anger leads to hate. Hate leads to suffering."
ANSWER

6 "Join me, and together we can rule the galaxy as father and son."
ANSWER

7 "Strike me down, and I will become more powerful than you could possibly imagine."
ANSWER

8 "I am a Jedi, like my father before me."
ANSWER

9 "At last we will reveal ourselves to the Jedi ... At last we will have revenge."
ANSWER

10 "Breep"
ANSWER

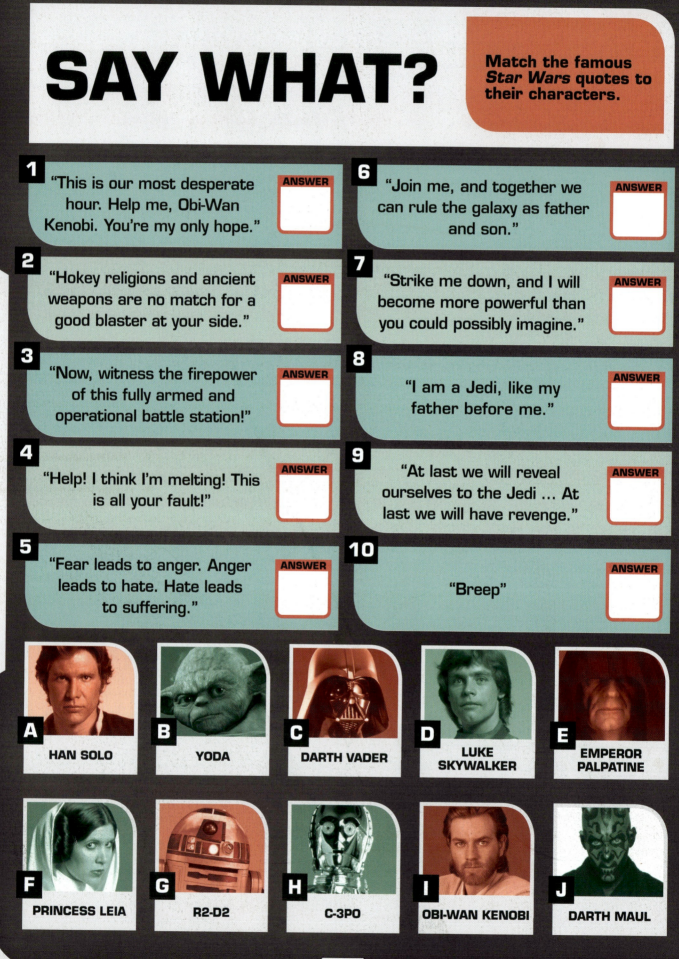

A HAN SOLO

B YODA

C DARTH VADER

D LUKE SKYWALKER

E EMPEROR PALPATINE

F PRINCESS LEIA

G R2-D2

H C-3PO

I OBI-WAN KENOBI

J DARTH MAUL

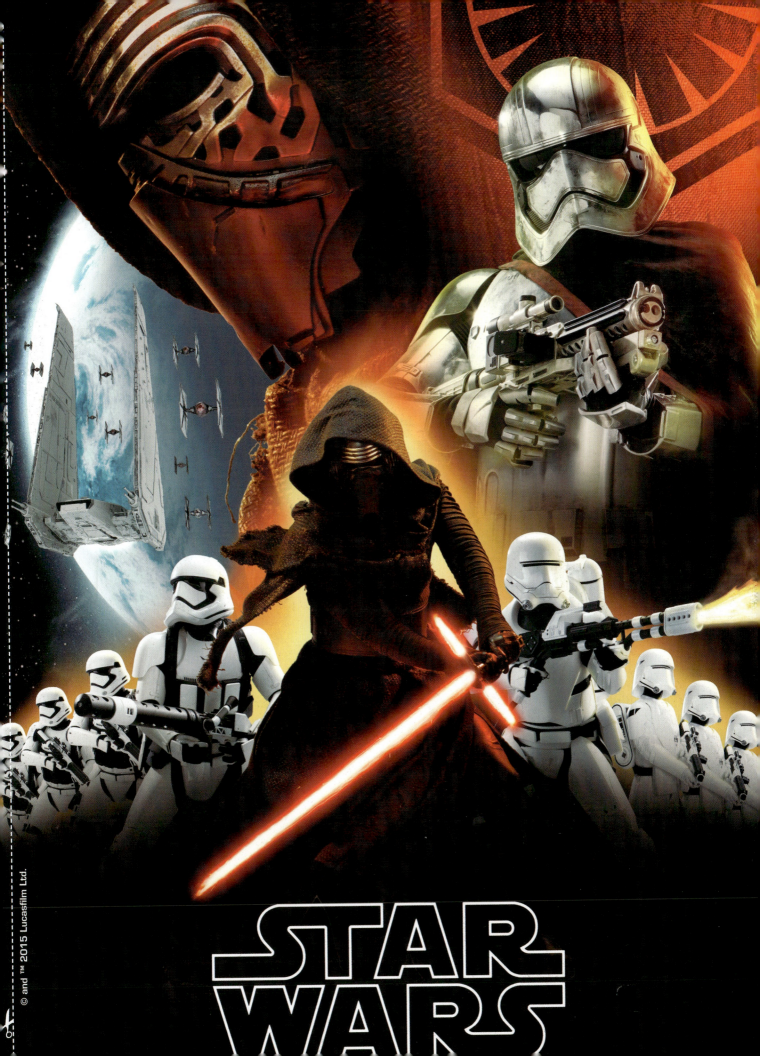

STAR WARS

3 GALACTIC MAGAZINES!

STAR WARS REBELS MAGAZINE

STAR WARS ADVENTURES

LEGO STAR WARS

ANSWERS

PAGE 9:

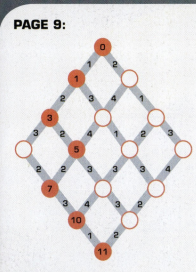

PAGE 24: LEIA

PAGE 25:

PAGE 35:

ACROSS
3: LANDO
5: NUTE
7: STORMTROOPERS
9: FEDERATION
11: SITH
14: RED
16: PHANTOM
17: DROID
18: CLONE
19: CLOUD

DOWN
1: MASTER
2: GON
4: AT-AT
6: AMIDALA
7: SMUGGLER
8: EWOKS
10: ALDERAAN
12: HATE
13: FORCE
15: ENDOR
16: PODRACING

PAGE 38:

YOU WILL GO TO THE
DAGOBAH SYSTEM. THERE YOU
WILL LEARN FROM YODA.

PAGE 39:

PAGE 46:

PAGE 47:

PAGE 48:

THE REBELS ARE AT THE
DOCKING BAY

PAGE 49:

PAGE 58:

1. F
2. A
3. E
4. H
5. B
6. C
7. I
8. D
9. J
10. G